This book belongs to

_____

Walt Disney® VOLUME 2

THUMPER'S
LITTLE SISTERS

WALT DISNEY FUN-TO-READ LIBRARY

A BANTAM BOOK
TORONTO • NEW YORK • LONDON • SYDNEY • AUCKLAND

Thumper's Little Sisters   A Bantam Book/January 1986   All rights reserved.   Copyright © 1986 The Walt Disney Company.   This book may not be reproduced, in whole or in part, by mimeograph or any other means.

ISBN 0-553-05574-7

Published simultaneously in the United States and Canada.   Bantam Books are published by Bantam Books, Inc.   Its trademark, consisting of the words "Bantam Books" and the portrayal of a rooster, is Registered in U.S. Patent and Trademark Office and in other countries.   Marca Registrada.   Bantam Books, Inc., 666 Fifth Avenue, New York, New York 10103.   Printed in the United States of America   0 9 8 7 6

One morning Thumper the rabbit felt sad.
He sat under a big oak tree. But he did not
thump his foot. He did not nibble the fresh
green grass. He just sat and looked sad.

"What's wrong, Thumper?" asked Bambi.
"My mother and father do not love me
anymore," said Thumper. "They hug my
baby sisters, but they never hug me. They
never talk to me. They have forgotten me!"

"Mothers and fathers never stop loving their children," said Bambi. "When your sisters are older, your mother and father will have more time for you. And your sisters will be more fun!"

Thumper felt happier when he heard this.
He went home right away.

But things did not get better. Things got worse.

When Thumper tried to thump in the house, his father stopped him.

"Quiet, Thumper! Your sisters are asleep!"

When Thumper tried to nibble some dry grass, his mother stopped him.

"Don't eat everything in the burrow," she said. "Save some for your little sisters."

As the days went by, the babies did get older. They followed Thumper everywhere. And they never stopped asking him things.

"Why are you doing that, Thumper?" they asked. "Can we do it too?"

They sat on Thumper when he took his
nap. One sister poked him in the eye.
"Are you in there, Thumper?" she cried.

At last the sisters were old enough to play outside <u>all</u> day. And who did they want to play with? Thumper, of course!

"Watch out for them, Thumper," said his mother. "Don't let them get hurt."

Thumper did not want to watch out for his sisters. He wanted to play by himself. He turned his back and climbed a fence. His sisters ran across the field.

All of a sudden Thumper heard a squeal.
"Thumper, help!" cried one of the sisters.
"Save us!" cried another.
A dog had come sniffing through the grass.
It was a big, hungry-looking dog.

"Oh, no!" cried Thumper.

He jumped down from the fence, and he ran right in front of the dog.

The dog forgot about the baby rabbits. He ran after Thumper.

Thumper ran across the field. The dog ran after him. Thumper ran faster and faster, but still the dog ran after him.

"I must run home!" Thumper said to himself. "If I don't, the dog will get me."

With that, Thumper ran as fast as he could. He ran straight into the rabbit hole. The dog barked and howled outside.

"Oh my goodness! Now the dog knows where we live," cried Thumper's mother. She hugged the baby sisters.

Soon a man came from the farm and took the dog away.

"He's gone! We are safe!" said Thumper.
"Not for long," said Thumper's father.
"That dog will come back. What have I always
told you about dogs?"

"Don't lead a dog to your burrow," said Thumper in a low voice.

"Papa, Thumper had to do it," said one of the sisters.

"He did it for us," said another.

But Thumper's mother and father were not listening. "We have to go and look for a new burrow," said Thumper's father.

"You children stay here," said Thumper's mother. "We will come back for you."

So Thumper's mother and father set out to find a new burrow.

Thumper watched them go. He felt sad and hurt and angry, all at the same time.

"All right for them!" he said. "They don't care about me. I don't belong here anymore. I'll go and find a burrow of my own. Then they will be sorry!" He started off.

The sisters ran after him.
"Stop!" cried one.
"We love you!" said another.
"We don't want you to go!" said the third.

Thumper did not look back. He made believe he did not hear his sisters.

They stayed close behind Thumper. He went deep into the woods.

The sisters were there when Thumper
saw a hole. It looked as if it might make a
good home for one small rabbit.

Thumper sniffed at the hole. He wanted
to see if any other animal lived there. Then
he moved a little closer to the hole.

SNAP!

Thumper felt his feet go out from under him. He felt himself bounce high in the air.

He was caught in a snare! He hung from a high branch. And no matter how he tried, he could not free himself!

Thumper's sisters tried to help him. One
little sister stood on the other little sisters. But
the branch was too high. They could not
reach Thumper.

"Don't be afraid, Thumper," said one sister.
"We'll get help," said the second.
The third sister stayed with Thumper. "I
will sing to you so that you won't be lonely,"
she said.

The first two sisters ran to get help.
The third sister sang a gentle little song.
She stayed close to Thumper.

Soon the two sisters came back. Bambi was with them. So was Flower the skunk.

Bambi tried to bend the tree so that it touched the ground. Then Thumper could wriggle free. Flower helped.

But before Thumper was free, his mother
and father came down the path.

"Oh, Thumper!" cried his mother. She was very frightened.

"Be brave, Thumper!" said his father. "We will save you!"

Bambi gave the tree branch a great tug.
Flower bounced on the branch as hard as
he could.

Thumper's sisters pulled and tugged at Thumper's ears.
At last Thumper's foot came out of the snare!

"Thumper dear!" said his mother. She hugged him until she took his breath away.

"We saved Thumper, Mama," said one of the sisters.
"And he saved us!" said another.

Then the sisters told the whole story of
how Thumper had run in front of the dog.
"That big old dog wanted to eat us up,"
they said. "But Thumper did not let him."

Thumper's father was so proud that he hardly knew what to do. "That's my boy!" he said. Then his father thumped Thumper on the back to show how proud he was.

Thumper was happy.

"My mother and father do love me," he
said. "They were just too busy to tell me."

"I guess mothers and fathers are like
that," said Bambi.

"My little sisters love me too," said
Thumper. "I'm glad I have little sisters. They
are not so bad after all!"

Then Thumper went off with his mother
and father and sisters, to find a new home.
And he never again thought that his mother
and father did not love him.

He knew that they did. They always
would, no matter how many young rabbits
there might be in the burrow.